A Donkey Called Mistletoe

HELEN PETERS

illustrated by
ELLIE SNOWDON

nosy
crow

Also by
HELEN PETERS

LOOK OUT FOR:

A Piglet Called Truffle

A Duckling Called Button

A Sheepdog Called Sky

A Kitten Called Holly

A Lamb Called Lucky

A Goat Called Willow

An Otter Called Pebble

An Owl Called Star

A Deer Called Dotty

FOR OLDER READERS:

The Secret Hen House Theatre

The Farm Beneath the Water

Evie's Ghost

Anna at War

For Kirsty and Fiona,
my wonderful editors.
H. P.

For Han x
E. S.

First published in the UK in 2020 by Nosy Crow Ltd
The Crow's Nest, 14 Baden Place, Crosby Row
London SE1 1YW

Nosy Crow and associated logos are trademarks and/or registered
trademarks of Nosy Crow Ltd

Text copyright © Helen Peters, 2020
Cover and illustrations copyright © Ellie Snowdon, 2020

The right of Helen Peters and Ellie Snowdon to be identified
as the author and illustrator respectively of this work has been asserted
by them in accordance with the Copyright, Designs
and Patents Act 1988.

ISBN: 978 1 78800 834 1

A CIP catalogue record for this book will be available from the British Library.

Printed and bound in Great Britain by Clays Ltd, Elcograf S.p.A.

Papers used by Nosy Crow are made from wood grown in sustainable forests.

MIX
Paper from
responsible sources
FSC
www.fsc.org   FSC® C018072

1 3 5 7 9 10 8 6 4 2
www.nosycrow.com

Chapter One
The Back End
of a Donkey

Jasmine and her best friend, Tom, were in the kitchen at Oak Tree Farm when Jasmine's little brother, Manu, flung the door open and ran in, dropping his coat and school bag on the floor.

"Guess what?" he said, an enormous grin on his face.

"What?" said Jasmine, glancing up from the chopping board. She was cutting up a carrot as a treat for Dotty, her pet deer. Dotty only had three legs, which meant she couldn't live in the wild, but she managed very well in the orchard.

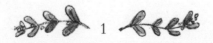

1

"Where's Dad?" asked Manu. "I want to tell you all together."

"In his office," said Jasmine.

Their dad was the farmer at Oak Tree Farm. He worked outdoors most of the time but he had an office in the house where he did all his paperwork.

"Oh, good," said Manu, running out of the room. "I'll go and get him. I've got the best news."

Jasmine's mum, Nadia, walked into the kitchen and hung up her car keys. Nadia was a vet, and she had collected Manu from his after-school football club on her way home from the surgery.

"Hey, you two," she said. "I bet you're happy it's Friday."

"Yep," said Jasmine. "We're going to spend lots of time with Dotty and Truffle this weekend. Try to cheer them up."

Truffle, Jasmine's pet pig, lived with Dotty in the orchard.

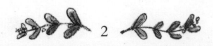

"Are they any better today, do you think?" asked Nadia.

"No," said Jasmine flatly. "They're still lying down all the time, and they've hardly touched their food."

Until last week, Jasmine's dad's elderly spaniel, Bramble, had lived in the orchard too. But Bramble hadn't been very well for the past few months, and on Monday she had died in her sleep.

Mum had tried to comfort Jasmine. "She was very old for a spaniel. And she had a lovely life. She got to spend every day running around the farm with Dad, and when she wasn't with him she had Truffle and Dotty to keep her company."

But Jasmine was inconsolable. She was very upset about Bramble, but she was even sadder for Truffle and Dotty. They always used to run and greet her every time she came to see them. Truffle would grunt with happiness and flop over to have her tummy tickled. Dotty would

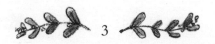

lick Jasmine's hand and nuzzle against her. But since Bramble had gone, they just lay on the grass all day. Truffle kept her head down and Dotty curled herself up into a ball. They didn't even look up when Jasmine approached. Most worrying of all, they showed no interest in food.

"We're giving them carrots and grapes," Tom told Nadia. "We tried apples, but they didn't want them."

Just then, Manu came back, dragging Dad by the hand.

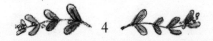

"So what's this amazing news, then?" asked Mum.

"We got told our parts in the nativity play," said Manu, "and guess what me and Ben are going to be?"

"Shepherds?" said Mum.

Manu grinned and shook his head. "No."

"Wise Men?" asked Dad.

Jasmine snorted. "Wise Men? Those two? As if."

"Angels?" said Mum, and everybody laughed.

"Sheep?" suggested Tom.

Manu smiled knowingly. "Getting closer."

"Cows?" said Tom. "Pigs?"

Jasmine shook her head. "They're not clever enough to be pigs."

Manu could contain himself no longer. "We're the donkey!" he burst out.

Dad roared with laughter. "Well, that makes perfect sense."

"Mrs Cowan's going to get an actual proper

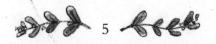

donkey costume," said Manu, looking as if he might burst with excitement. "Ben's going to be the front legs and the head and I'm going to be the back legs."

"Well, this is definitely an event that will need to be recorded," said Dad. "We must make sure we get front-row seats."

"We're doing a special performance for the old people in Holly Tree House the week before we do the one for the parents. And we're going to have tea with the old people after the play," said Manu. "Everyone's going to sing 'Little Donkey' when me and Ben come in. Except Harrison. He won't sing. He doesn't even want to be in the play."

Harrison was a new boy in Manu's class. Manu and his best friend, Ben, had made friends with him straightaway. Jasmine's family had heard a lot about Harrison lately. He liked things to be calm and orderly, and he got stressed and upset if people were noisy and boisterous. So it was very

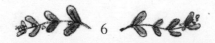

strange, Jasmine thought, that Harrison would want to be friends with her brother. But the boys had bonded over a shared love of bugs, and now they seemed to spend most of their playtimes making homes for insects on the school field.

"Can Harrison come round to ours?" asked Manu. "He says there'll be loads of good bugs here, because of all the dung."

"I like the sound of Harrison," said Dad. "Not everybody appreciates the finer qualities of farm manure."

"Of course he can come," said Nadia. "I'll text his mum."

"Will Ella be home in time for the play?" said Manu. "I really want her to see it."

Ella was Jasmine and Manu's older sister, and she was away at university.

"I'm sure she'll be there if she can," said Mum. "I can't believe my son's going to be the back end of a donkey. I've never been more proud."

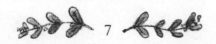

Chapter Two
Meeting Mistletoe

On Saturday morning, Tom and Jasmine took grapes and pears out to the orchard. Truffle ate half-heartedly. Dotty just sniffed the pieces and turned away.

Jasmine sighed. "Look at her sad eyes. I don't think she'll ever feel better."

"It's only been a week," said Tom. "Your mum said they should improve soon."

"But what if they don't? What if they carry on refusing to eat?"

"Do you think your dad will get another

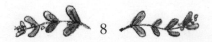

dog?" asked Tom.

Jasmine shook her head. "Manu wants a puppy, but Dad said no because of Sky."

Sky was a collie that Jasmine had rescued as a puppy. He belonged to her, but because he was a sheepdog, he spent a lot of time on the farm with Dad.

"And Mum says we've got more than enough pets as it is," said Jasmine.

As well as Truffle, Dotty and Sky, Jasmine had two cats called Toffee and Marmite, a tame duck called Button and a sheep called Lucky. Button lived with the chickens in the farmyard and Lucky lived with the other sheep in the field, though, so they didn't make any extra work.

When the children went in for lunch, Jasmine's dad said, "I'm going to do a few jobs for Mr Hobson at Honey Farm this afternoon. Would you two like to come along?"

"Can we meet his donkey?" asked Jasmine.

"Of course," said Dad.

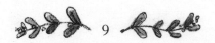

"Then we'll come," said Jasmine. "Won't we, Tom?"

"Definitely," said Tom.

Dad had told Jasmine about Mr Hobson. He lived close to Oak Tree Farm. He was very old now, and Dad had recently started helping him out with odd jobs. Mr Hobson had had to sell most of his animals, but he had kept Mistletoe, his pet donkey.

When they got to Honey Farm, Dad introduced Jasmine and Tom to the old farmer.

"Mistletoe's very friendly," Mr Hobson said. "He'll love you making a fuss of him. Just approach him from the side, and talk to him as you approach, so you don't startle him."

Jasmine and Tom left the men to chat and walked across the yard to Mistletoe's field. Tom had brought a carrot for him and Jasmine had an apple, which they carried in their pockets. They stopped at the gate and scanned the field.

"There he is!" said Tom, pointing.

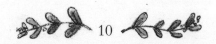

At the far end of the meadow, near a wooden barn, a small brown donkey was looking over the fence into the next field, where two floppy-eared goats and a group of hens were gathered.

"Come on," said Jasmine, climbing over the gate.

In the middle of the field they passed a single tree. Its branches were bare, but a huge clump of mistletoe, with bright-green leaves and fat pearly-white berries, hung from a high branch.

"Look!" said Tom. "I wonder if that's how the donkey got his name."

"Hello, Mistletoe," said Jasmine, as they slowly approached. "How are you today?"

Mistletoe had deep-brown eyes and a patient, gentle expression. His fur was all brown except for the tip of his nose, which was pure white, and a long black cross on his back.

"He's lovely," said Tom, stroking the donkey's dark mane. "He's got such a kind-looking face. And beautiful eyes."

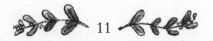

"He looks very thoughtful, doesn't he," said Jasmine, patting Mistletoe's flank.

"Huge ears," said Tom, stroking the long pointed ears, brown on the outside and white on the inside, that stood straight up on the top of the donkey's head, facing attentively forward. Mistletoe nuzzled his arm.

"Look, he really likes me," said Tom.

Jasmine laughed. "I think he can smell the carrot."

Sure enough, the donkey started to nuzzle the pocket of Tom's coat. "You'll have to move your head away, Mistletoe," said Tom, "or I won't be able to get it."

Jasmine took the apple from her pocket and, holding it out with her palm really flat, offered it to Mistletoe. He snatched it up and crunched noisily. When he finished, he started nuzzling Jasmine's pocket again. Tom held the carrot towards him. The donkey grabbed it and Tom hastily let go as Mistletoe pulled the whole thing

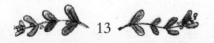

into his mouth. He crunched it contentedly as Jasmine and Tom stroked his soft fur.

"He seems really peaceful," said Tom.

Suddenly Mistletoe lifted his head, pricked up his ears and looked towards the farmyard. Jasmine and Tom followed his gaze and saw Mr Hobson driving across the yard on his special all-terrain mobility scooter. The donkey brayed so loudly that Jasmine and Tom laughed in surprise. They followed him as he trotted to the gate to greet his friend.

Mr Hobson opened the gate and drove into the field. The mobility scooter had big tyres for driving across rough ground. Tom looked at it enviously.

Mistletoe put his nose in Mr Hobson's lap. The farmer stroked him.

"How are you this morning, old boy? Have you been behaving yourself for these two?"

"He's been perfect," said Jasmine. "And he really liked the treats."

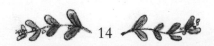 14

Mr Hobson laughed. "I bet he did. He loves his food, this one. He's getting too fat, having all this grass to himself."

"Does he like those goats and chickens?" asked Tom.

"He seems to. He spends a lot of time looking at them over the fence. I think he's been lonely since I had to sell the sheep. Donkeys are very sociable, so if they don't have another donkey around, they'll look for other animals to bond with."

"How old is he?" asked Tom.

"Nearly twenty. I've had him since he was a foal."

Tom looked alarmed. Bramble had been fifteen when she died.

Mr Hobson saw the look on Tom's face. "Don't worry, twenty isn't that old for a donkey. They generally live to thirty, and some of them go on until fifty."

"Did you ever ride him?" asked Jasmine.

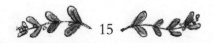

"No, I got him to protect the lambs against foxes. Donkeys are good guard animals for sheep. But he's always been more of a pet, really. And he's too old to start being ridden now."

"Is it true that all donkeys have a black cross on their backs?" asked Tom.

"Every donkey in the whole world. There's a legend that says it's because of their connection with Jesus. One version says the donkey who carried Jesus into Jerusalem on Palm Sunday went and stood beside him on his cross, and the shadow of the cross fell across the donkey's back and shoulders. But some scientists think it's for camouflage, the same way that tigers' stripes help them blend into their surroundings."

"He's so lovely," said Tom, stroking Mistletoe's mane.

"He's the sweetest donkey you could ever hope to meet," said Mr Hobson. "I'm really going to miss him."

"What do you mean?" said Jasmine.

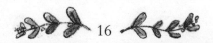 16

Mr Hobson sighed. "I was just telling your dad. It's got to the point where I can't look after him properly, and it's not fair on Mistletoe. I pay a girl to help out, but it's not much of a life for him. He loves company, and he's spending too much time on his own."

"So what are you going to do?" asked Jasmine.

"Well, I'm moving into Holly Tree House next month," said Mr Hobson. Holly Tree House was the old people's home in the village. "I've finally had to face the fact that I can't really manage on my own any more. It's very nice of your dad and other people to come and help out, but they're all busy and I don't want to be a burden."

Jasmine couldn't think of anything to say. It seemed so awful that Mr Hobson thought of himself as a burden.

"And Mistletoe will go to the animal sanctuary in Latchford," he said. "They rang me this morning to say they can collect him in two weeks' time."

"But isn't that miles away?" said Tom.

"It's a fair distance. I don't expect I'll ever see him again."

The old man looked so sad that Jasmine couldn't bear it.

"But me and Tom have got an animal sanctuary," she said. "On our farm."

Mr Hobson looked at her in surprise. So did Tom.

"Well, we do," said Jasmine, seeing Tom's look. "I mean, we're going to have an animal sanctuary when we're grown up. But we already do, really. We've rescued loads of animals."

This was true. As well as the animals that had stayed on the farm, Jasmine and Tom had rescued a baby goat, a kitten, two sparrow chicks, an otter cub and a barn owl.

"But you're not allowed any more pets," said Tom.

Jasmine glared at him. "Yes, I am."

She smiled at Mr Hobson. "Honestly, we'd

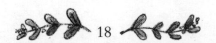

love to have Mistletoe. And then you could come and see him all the time."

Mr Hobson patted her hand. "You're very kind, but you mustn't worry. I'm sure he'll be well looked after. Now, tell me all about your animals. Your dad says you've got a deer in the orchard. How's she getting on?"

"She was doing really well until Dad's spaniel died last week. Bramble was like a mum to Dotty, and now Dotty's pining for her. So's Truffle, my pig. They all lived together, you see."

Jasmine and Tom talked with Mr Hobson until they had to leave. As they walked to Dad's truck, Jasmine turned to look back at the old man and the donkey. Mistletoe had laid his head in Mr Hobson's lap. Mr Hobson was scratching Mistletoe's ears and speaking to him softly. And then Jasmine saw something that sent a stab of pain to her heart.

Mr Hobson's eyes were full of tears.

Chapter Three
A Donkey Sleepover

Back at Oak Tree Farm, Tom and Jasmine sat
side by side on Jasmine's bed. She had her mum's
laptop and Tom had her dad's.

"We need to research everything about donkey
care," she said. "Then we can show Mum and
Dad we know all about donkeys and they'll let
Mistletoe come and live here."

"But your parents won't let you have him.
You've only just got Dotty, and they said no
more animals."

"That's the whole point, though, isn't it? Dotty

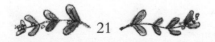

and Truffle are missing Bramble, and Mistletoe will be missing Mr Hobson. So they can all make friends, and then they'll cheer each other up."

Tom looked thoughtful. "That might work. He seemed to like those goats and chickens in the next field. OK, so let's find out how to look after donkeys."

The first thing he discovered was that, unlike horses, donkeys don't have a waterproof coating on their fur.

"So they need to be able to shelter from the rain. But there isn't a barn in the orchard, so he couldn't live with Dotty and Truffle."

Dotty and Truffle slept in Bramble's kennel. It was a big kennel, but not big enough for a donkey.

Jasmine was looking at Tom's screen. "It says a three-sided shelter is fine. Dad could build one. He's good at building stuff. And it could be my Christmas present."

Tom carried on reading. "It says they should

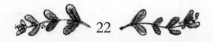

eat mainly barley straw, because it's high in fibre and low in sugar, and it's close to what they would eat in the wild."

"That's perfect! We always have loads of barley straw for the cows and sheep."

"And they need a mineral lick."

"He's got one," said Jasmine. "I saw it in the barn. So we could take that with us. I could ask for another one for Christmas. The one he's got should last until then."

"Apart from that, they just need clean water, and they browse for food in the fields," said Tom. "It says it's good for them to share a field with other animals."

"For company?"

"Well, mainly because they get fat if they have too much grass. But they do need company too, which is perfect for Dotty and Truffle."

Jasmine raised her eyebrows at him. "See, you like the idea now, don't you?"

"Well, it would be really nice having them all

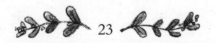

living together. And donkeys don't seem that hard to look after."

"It says here they need their hooves trimmed by a farrier every six to ten weeks, to stop them getting overgrown," said Jasmine. "I don't know how much that costs. But if I ask all my relatives for money for Christmas, hopefully I'll get enough to pay for the farrier's visits until my birthday."

Tom looked worried. "How are we actually going to do this, though? If Mistletoe's living in the orchard, we can't exactly keep it a secret."

"I'm not asking my parents," said Jasmine. "You know what they're like. They always say no to everything."

"So what are you going to do, then?"

"Mr Hobson's happy for us to have him, isn't he? He said so."

Tom frowned. "No, he didn't."

"He said it was very kind of me to offer, but not to worry. That's what people always say when they want you to do something but they're too polite to say so. Obviously he'd like us to have him."

"But we still can't keep him secretly."

"No, but we can bring him here without telling them first. And then he'll make friends with Dotty and Truffle, and once Mum and Dad see them all snuggled up happily together, they'll change their minds and let me keep him."

"But what if they don't? Or what if the animals don't like each other? Then we'd have to tell Mr Hobson we couldn't have him after all,

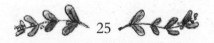

and that wouldn't be fair."

Jasmine sighed impatiently. But Tom was thinking. After a pause, he said, "How about we ask Mr Hobson if we can bring Mistletoe here for a trial, to see how he gets on with the other animals? We could just ask to bring him for one night."

"Like a donkey sleepover!" said Jasmine.

"Exactly. Then once he's here we can try and persuade your parents to let us keep him. And if they won't, then we'll just have to take him back and he'll go to the animal sanctuary, like Mr Hobson's arranged anyway."

Jasmine nodded thoughtfully. "That is actually a good plan." She shut the laptop and stood up. "Let's find his number and phone him right now."

Chapter Four
Withers and Fetlocks

Unfortunately, Mr Hobson didn't think a donkey sleepover was a good idea. Not yet, anyway.

"Why don't you come and spend some time with him first?" he said. "I can show you what he needs and you can get to know him better."

"That would be great," said Jasmine, trying to hide her disappointment about the sleepover. "Can we come tomorrow?"

So they spent Sunday morning with Dotty and Truffle, and then walked across the fields to Honey Farm after lunch. When they arrived, Mr

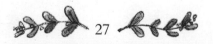

Hobson was in the field on his mobility scooter, stroking Mistletoe's neck.

"Thank you for helping out," he said. "I'm very grateful to you."

"We're very grateful to you," said Jasmine.

Mr Hobson laughed. "You might not say that once you find out what you've got to do. The first job is mucking out and picking up the dung."

"We don't mind," said Jasmine. "We want to do all the jobs."

Tom mucked out the barn while Jasmine trundled a wheelbarrow around the field, picking up dung with a manure scoop. She was hoping Mistletoe might follow her, but he stayed by Mr Hobson's side the whole time.

When they finished, Mr Hobson said, "I expect you'd like to groom him, wouldn't you?"

Jasmine and Tom grinned at each other.

"Can you bring his head collar from the barn, then?"

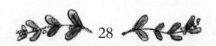

28

Jasmine fetched the collar and lead rope from the hook on the barn wall.

"He's used to wearing it," said Mr Hobson, "but he needs to get used to you putting it on, so go slow. Talk to him quietly and take a bit of time to scratch his withers first, so he relaxes with you."

"Scratch his what?" said Tom.

Jasmine wasn't entirely sure what the withers were either, but she would never have admitted it.

Mr Hobson indicated the point at the top of the donkey's shoulders, just below his mane.

"That's called his withers. Donkeys like being scratched there, and on their ears and back."

Jasmine scratched Mistletoe's withers while Tom stroked his ears.

"That's right," said Mr Hobson. "You can see he's relaxed when he's standing nice and quietly like this and his ears are pointing forwards. If he flattens his ears back, or swishes his tail or stamps

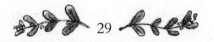

his foot, those are all warning signs that he's uneasy about something."

"What should we do if he does that?" asked Tom.

"Just stand there quietly, and when he stops swishing or stamping, move away a bit. Never try to force a donkey to do anything. They respond to rewards, so if he does something well, stroke or scratch him."

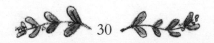

"What about treats?" asked Jasmine.

Mr Hobson shook his head. "Bribing donkeys with food encourages all sorts of bad behaviour. They might just snatch it and run away, or even bite you to try to get a treat. The best reward is to give him attention. Now he's nice and relaxed, so you can hold the collar in front of him and let him sniff it."

Mistletoe happily sniffed the collar. Mr Hobson showed the children how to fit it and attach the lead rope to the ring under his chin.

"There you go. Now you can give him a scratch before you start grooming him."

"Do you groom him every day?" asked Jasmine.

"Generally we do. It's a good way to check for any skin problems or injuries as well as keeping him clean, and it helps you bond with him. We don't groom him if his coat's wet, though, because the water and dirt get to the skin, and that means more chance of infection."

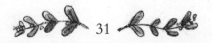

Tom fetched the box of combs and brushes from the barn. Mr Hobson placed it on his knees.

"Start with the dandy brush. One of you can hold the lead rope while the other one grooms him."

"You can brush him first if you want," Jasmine said to Tom, feeling very generous.

"Use the dandy brush to get dried mud and dirt off," said Mr Hobson. "It's got hard bristles, so don't use it on his lower legs, face or ears, where he's more sensitive."

Tom put his hand on Mistletoe's neck and said, "I'm just going to brush your back, OK?"

"That's exactly right," said Mr Hobson approvingly. "Always keep a hand on him as you're working your way round, so he knows where you are, and keep talking to him. And walk around the front of him, not the rear. He's very unlikely to kick, but you never know when something might startle him."

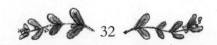 32

When Tom had finished, he held the rope while Jasmine used the soft-bristled body brush on Mistletoe's ears, face, belly, tail and lower legs, talking reassuringly to him the whole time.

Mr Hobson showed them how to clean the dirt out of the brushes with the plastic curry comb. Then he handed the hoof pick to Jasmine.

"His hooves need picking out every day. He's very quiet generally, but if he's in pain, or he senses you're nervous, he might kick out, so go carefully. Start by running your hand from his withers down his front left shoulder, then down the back of his leg to the fetlock joint."

Jasmine wasn't sure what the fetlock joint was, so she ran her hand slowly down Mistletoe's leg, hoping Mr Hobson would tell her where to stop. When her hand was almost at the bottom of his leg, Mr Hobson said, "Now tug gently at the fetlock to encourage him to pick his foot up."

So a fetlock is basically an ankle, Jasmine thought.

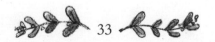

She pulled gently. Mistletoe kept his foot on the ground. She tried again but he still didn't budge.

"If he doesn't want to move, lean against his shoulder with your hip," said Mr Hobson. "That usually does the trick. It shifts his weight to the other foot, you see."

Jasmine leaned heavily against Mistletoe and grasped his fetlock again. This time, he picked up his foot.

Good," said Mr Hobson. "Now, don't lift it too high, and keep his foot directly under his body – you don't want to put any strain on his joints."

Following his instructions, Jasmine picked out the mud and small stones from Mistletoe's front feet. Then she held the rope while Tom did the back ones.

"If you do that every day," said Mr Hobson, "you get to know how his feet should look, and you'll be able to spot any injuries or swellings early on."

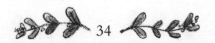

34

"It's so much work looking after a donkey,"
said Tom in amazement. "I always thought they
just lived in a field and that was it."

Mr Hobson smiled. "Are you changing your
minds?"

"No!" they said, shaking their heads
emphatically.

Tom was right, Jasmine thought. It was a lot of
work. But that just made it more exciting. She
couldn't wait to take Mistletoe home with her.

Chapter Five
One Crucial Question

When Tom and Jasmine had finished grooming Mistletoe, Mr Hobson showed them how to lead him around the field on a slack rope. They had to say, "Walk on," when they wanted him to move and, "Stand," to get him to stop.

Jasmine was getting more and more excited at the thought of bringing Mistletoe to Oak Tree Farm. But first there was one crucial question to be answered. Would Mistletoe get on with Dotty and Truffle?

As they unfastened his head collar, Jasmine

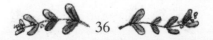

had an idea.

"Would it be OK to come again next Saturday and bring Dotty with us? To introduce her to Mistletoe?"

Mr Hobson smiled at her. "Is this part of your scheme to have Mistletoe living at your farm?"

"Yes. He'd be living in the orchard with Dotty and Truffle, you see."

"And what do your mum and dad think about this?"

"I haven't exactly told them yet," said Jasmine. "We want to make sure the animals get on first."

"Well, by all means bring Dotty on Saturday. I'd love to meet her."

"Can we bring my dog as well? He's very well behaved."

"Of course. I'd love to meet him too."

"It's just that Dotty's so depressed at the moment, she might refuse to come on her own. But if Sky's coming, she'll probably come too."

"Why don't you make a little pen for the

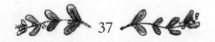

deer?" said Mr Hobson. "Then she and Mistletoe can get to know each other, but she'll be safe if Mistletoe takes against her for any reason."

Tom and Jasmine fetched four metal hurdles from the farmyard and constructed a little pen at the edge of the field. Jasmine called Mistletoe over to join them, but instead he walked to Mr Hobson and nuzzled into his shoulder. Mr Hobson leaned his head against the donkey's and closed his eyes.

A horrible wave of guilt flooded over Jasmine. She had been so excited about having Mistletoe that she had barely thought about how sad it would be for him and Mr Hobson to be parted. How selfish she was.

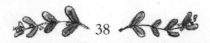

She was still feeling terrible when her mum and Manu appeared at the gate.

"Why are you here?" asked Jasmine.

"Charming," said Nadia. "Tom's going to his aunty's house, and I have to go shopping, so I said I'd pick you both up."

They dropped Tom at his aunty's house and then drove to the supermarket. Jasmine and Manu headed for the toy aisle while Nadia did the grocery shopping.

"Oh, look!" said Manu. "It's Harrison."

Manu's friend, Harrison, was sitting cross-legged on the floor in the middle of the aisle. His hands were clamped over his ears, his eyes were screwed shut and he was rocking to and fro, making loud moaning noises. His mum stood nearby, rummaging in her bag, looking tense and anxious.

Jasmine had seen Harrison do this in the school playground. It was how he reacted when things got too stressful for him.

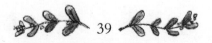

"Hey, Harrison," she said. "Are you OK?"

Harrison curled himself into a ball and carried on moaning.

Mum appeared at the end of the aisle. She looked puzzled at the sight of Jasmine crouching next to a small boy. Then she smiled as she recognised Harrison's mum. She walked towards her.

"How can I help, Sarah? Shall I get your shopping, then you can take Harrison home?"

Sarah forced a smile. "Thank you. I just need to sort out his headphones."

She set her bag on the ground and pulled out a pair of headphones and a phone. She tapped at the phone, then crouched next to Harrison and held out the headphones.

"Harrison," she said softly. "Do you want your headphones? Would you like your rainforest sounds or sea sounds?"

Harrison stopped moaning for a second and said, "Rainforest." He hovered his hands away from his ears to allow Sarah to put the headphones on. Then she took a little book about bugs from her bag and placed it gently in his hand. Harrison opened his eyes. His moaning had calmed and he was only rocking very slightly now.

Sarah took a deep breath and let it out in a long sigh.

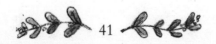

"Can I help with anything?" Nadia asked.

"No, thanks, I'm all done." Sarah indicated her basket. "I shouldn't have risked coming in, but we were on our way home and there were a few things I needed. It was OK until a group of kids jostled past and knocked him. That was too much for him, when he was already stressed."

"I hope Manu isn't too noisy for him," said Nadia, glancing at Manu, who was looking over Harrison's shoulder at a picture of a beetle.

"Harrison doesn't mind," said Sarah. "He likes making bug habitats with Manu and Ben. He just walks away if they get to be too much for him."

"I don't blame him," said Jasmine. "That's what I do, too."

Chapter Six
Getting to Know
Each Other

On the following Saturday afternoon, Jasmine
and Tom set out for Honey Farm with Dotty
and Sky. The collie bounded across the fields,
wagging his tail and running in big circles
around the children. Dotty walked on her lead
beside Jasmine. As Jasmine had predicted, she had
been reluctant to come: so reluctant, in fact,
that Jasmine had had to carry her out of the
orchard, while Sky leapt around her and gave
her some encouraging barks and licks to get her
going.

Mr Hobson and Mistletoe were at the far end of the field when they arrived. Tom tied Sky to the gatepost outside. "Good boy," he said. "Stay there."

Sky lay down contentedly, and Jasmine led Dotty to the pen. Mr Hobson drove across the field to greet them.

"What a beautiful little deer," he said, stroking Dotty's face. "She's a real credit to you, Jasmine."

"Thank you," said Jasmine, gazing at Dotty with pride. "She's too skinny at the moment, though. She's been off her food since Bramble died."

"Should we bring Mistletoe to meet her?" asked Tom.

Mr Hobson shook his head. "Best to let him do it in his own time."

So Jasmine got on with the mucking-out and Tom did the poo-picking, while Mistletoe browsed in the hedge at the top of the field. Dotty stood at the bars of the pen, making her

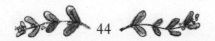

little bleating call to Jasmine now and again. Jasmine hoped Mistletoe would want to meet Dotty, but he didn't even seem to have noticed her.

Just as they finished their jobs, a middle-aged man walked into the field. He wore very new-looking jeans with smart shoes and a flowery shirt. He didn't look like a farmer.

"Dad!" he called, and Mr Hobson turned and drove across the field to meet him. Jasmine and Tom stared in fascination at Mr Hobson's son. He looked so different from his father.

Jasmine couldn't hear what he said, but she did hear Mr Hobson say, "Yes, that's fine. Do what you like with it. Don't fuss, I'll be in later."

His son said something else that Jasmine couldn't hear, and then he strode back towards the house, frowning. Jasmine glanced at Tom, and she could tell he felt awkward too.

They walked over to Mr Hobson.

"If you need to go in, it's OK," said Jasmine.

"We know what to do now."

He smiled at her. "I know you do. But it's a good excuse to keep out of the way while my children pack up the house. I've told them I don't care about any of it except the books and pictures, but they will keep fussing."

"Look!" whispered Tom.

Mistletoe had left the hedge and was ambling towards Dotty's pen. Jasmine held her breath as the old donkey approached the hurdles and stared at the little deer. Dotty stared back at him for several seconds. Then she leaned her long neck towards him until their faces were nearly touching. She sniffed. Mistletoe sniffed back.

Mr Hobson smiled. "That's good. They're getting to know each other."

The children walked Sky around the edge of the field on his lead, to give Dotty and Mistletoe time to bond. When they got back to Dotty's pen, Mistletoe had his head over the hurdles. They watched as Dotty leaned towards him and

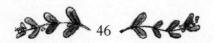

licked the side of his nose. The donkey stretched
his head further into the pen and Dotty licked
him again.

"They've started bonding!" said Jasmine. "Do you think we could let Dotty out of the pen?"

"Try it," said Mr Hobson. "I think they'll get on fine."

Jasmine opened the pen and fastened Dotty's lead to her collar. To her surprise and delight, Mistletoe turned and walked beside them as she led Dotty across the field. Tom and Sky walked on the other side of Mistletoe.

"Why don't you let Sky have a run off the lead?" suggested Mr Hobson. "He and Mistletoe don't seem bothered by each other."

Sky was delighted to be free. He bounded around the field, sniffing at every new scent, his tail wagging in delight. Mistletoe stayed with Dotty.

"Let the deer off the lead too, if you like," said Mr Hobson. So they did, but Dotty didn't run off like Sky. She stayed next to Mistletoe, matching his pace. She looked happier than she had done since Bramble had died.

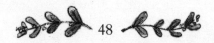

"That's amazing," said Tom. "She's attached to him already."

"I think she can sense something in Mistletoe that's like Bramble," said Jasmine. "Like Mistletoe has the same sort of soul as Bramble. Calm and gentle."

"Perhaps she likes being with an older animal," said Mr Hobson. "Like a sort of parent figure."

"Do you know if Mistletoe gets on with pigs? He'd be living with Truffle too."

"I don't think he's ever met a pig. But I've never had a problem with him getting on with any animal."

"I don't think we can bring Truffle here, though," said Jasmine. "She used to go for walks when she was younger, but she doesn't any more."

"How about you take Mistletoe to your place, then?" asked Mr Hobson. "For your sleepover thing. Give him a bit more lead training now, then you should be fine to walk him over the

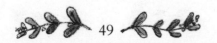

fields tomorrow."

Tom and Jasmine beamed in delight. "That would be amazing!" said Jasmine.

"You'll have to ask your parents first, though," said Mr Hobson. "I don't want them telling me off for letting you take a donkey home without their permission."

Chapter Seven
Like a
Bucking Bronco

"Ted Hobson phoned to say how helpful you
and Tom have been," said Dad at dinnertime.
"Sounds like he's enjoyed having you around."

Jasmine knew a good chance when she saw
it. "He said we can walk Mistletoe over here
tomorrow. It's very good for donkeys to go for
walks and get new stimulation."

Mum frowned. "Are you sure you'll be able to
manage him by yourselves?"

Manu looked excited. "Me and Ben can
practise his walk and copy his noises, and then

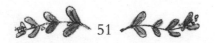

when we get the costume we'll be exactly like a real donkey."

"Can we ride him, too?" asked Ben, who had come to have tea with Manu.

Manu's eyes lit up. "Let's have a rodeo! If I got on him and kicked my heels, I bet he'd gallop."

"You can't ride him," said Jasmine. "He's old and he's never been ridden. He might throw you off."

Ben laughed. "Like a bucking bronco!"

"He couldn't throw *me* off," said Manu, "even if he got right up on his hind legs. I'd just hold on to his mane, and even if he was kicking and going crazy, I wouldn't fall off."

"You fell off the bucking bronco at the school fair," said Ben. "You only stayed on it for about two seconds."

"That wasn't my fault. The man didn't give me a chance to get on properly before he started it up."

"You fell off on your second go, too. And your

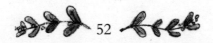

third go. And—"

"Anyway, you're not riding him," said Jasmine, "so don't even think about it." She turned to her father. "Dad, can me and Tom fence off a bit of the orchard?"

"What for?"

"Just so Mistletoe can rest there. We don't want to leave him tied up, but we can't let him loose with Truffle, in case they don't get on. He's going to be here all day while Mr Hobson's clearing out his house."

"Poor Mr Hobson," said Mum. "It must be terrible, having to leave his home."

"Especially when he's leaving Mistletoe too," said Jasmine. "And the animal sanctuary's so far away that they won't ever see each other again."

Mum gave her a stern look. "I know what you're trying to do, Jasmine, but you know perfectly well what the answer is."

"I thought Dotty was looking more perky this afternoon," said Dad, trying to change the subject.

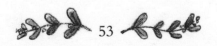

"That's because we took her to see Mistletoe," said Jasmine. "You wouldn't believe how well they get on. Imagine how happy she'd be if he could stay here forever."

Jasmine felt tremendous pride as they led the old donkey across the fields on Sunday morning. He walked calmly beside them, his ears forward. Tom held the leading rein and Jasmine carried the box of brushes and equipment.

"He really trusts us, doesn't he?" said Tom. "He's quite happy with us leading him."

Dad had helped them put a fence across the orchard. Dotty and Truffle were in the top half, and the children led Mistletoe through the garden gate into the bottom half. They had filled a feed bowl with fresh barley straw.

"He'll love browsing in the hedge," said Jasmine. "There's so much tasty stuff there."

Dotty and Truffle were lying under an apple tree. As Mistletoe walked into the orchard,

Dotty raised her head. She gave an excited bleat and scrabbled to her feet. Mistletoe brayed in greeting and Tom unclipped the lead rope.

The fence was no barrier for the little deer. She leapt it easily and ran towards the donkey. She stopped in front of him and he dipped his head so she could nuzzle his face.

"What a lovely sight!"

Tom and Jasmine turned to see Nadia standing at the gate.

Jasmine beamed. "See how they love each other. We think Dotty's adopted Mistletoe as a kind of replacement for Bramble."

Dotty set off at a trot around the orchard. To Jasmine's amazement, Mistletoe started to trot after her.

"Look how happy they are! And Dotty's been so miserable. It's like they were made for each other."

Mum sighed. "They're very lovely together. I can absolutely see that. But you can't just carry on accumulating animals forever."

"Why not?"

"Well, for one thing, the expense. There's the cost of putting up a decent shelter. And donkeys need regular farrier's visits, did you know that?"

"Yes," said Jasmine. "I'm going to ask everyone for money for Christmas and birthdays. And—"

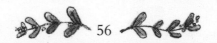

A
Donkey
Called
Mistletoe

Mum's phone rang. She took it out of her pocket and looked at the screen.

"Sorry, I need to get this. But the answer is still no." She walked back towards the house.

"She's not going to change her mind, is she?" said Tom. "I mean, if she wasn't even convinced by seeing them together like that, what will it take to convince her?"

Mistletoe and Dotty spent the whole morning together, grazing and browsing, occasionally kicking up their heels and going for a trot around the orchard. Jasmine kept hoping that Mistletoe and Truffle would start to make friends, but they took no notice at all of each other.

Manu was very excited to meet Mistletoe, but he soon grew restless when the donkey wasn't as lively as he'd hoped.

"Why doesn't he gallop? I thought he'd be galloping all the time."

'He's an old donkey," said Jasmine. "And it's not a rodeo."

"He's a boring donkey," said Manu.

He left the orchard. A few minutes later, he was back. "Mum wants you in the kitchen."

Jasmine frowned. "What for?"

"Dunno. She said she needs to talk to you right now. And Tom."

Tom looked worried. "What have we done?"

"I don't know," said Jasmine. Her mind went over all her recent crimes. "Maybe she knows it was us who ate that whole packet of biscuits. But she doesn't usually make a fuss about stuff like that."

Mum was in the kitchen, answering emails on her laptop.

"What do you want us for?" asked Jasmine.

Mum looked up, a puzzled expression on her face. "What do you mean?"

"Manu said you wanted to see us."

Mum frowned. "I didn't say that."

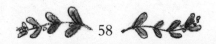

At the exact same moment, Tom and Jasmine
gasped. They stared at each other, each seeing
their own thoughts mirrored in the other's face.
Without a word, they turned and ran.

It was exactly as Jasmine had feared. As soon
as they came within sight of the orchard, she
saw Manu trying to scramble on to Mistletoe.
He almost had one leg over the donkey's back,
and he was frantically trying to hoist himself
upright. Mistletoe's ears were flattened
back, and he was swishing his tail
and stamping.

For a moment, Jasmine stood frozen in panic. Then she started running, her heart thumping in her chest, praying Mistletoe wouldn't bolt before she got to Manu. As she reached the orchard gate, Manu started slithering off Mistletoe's back. In a desperate attempt to stay on, he grabbed the donkey's mane in both fists. Mistletoe threw up his head and brayed loudly. He kicked up his heels and galloped across the orchard. Manu screamed as he was dragged across the grass, one hand still clutching Mistletoe's mane.

Jasmine raced into the orchard. But before she could reach Manu, Nadia, with what seemed like superhuman speed, sprinted past her.

"Let go!" Nadia shouted, running alongside Mistletoe and grabbing Manu around the waist. "I've got you!"

Manu let go and Nadia pulled him away. The donkey continued to gallop around the orchard, braying and tossing his head. Nadia led Manu into the garden. Jasmine followed, shutting the

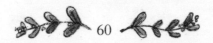

60

gate behind her. Manu was wide-eyed and his teeth were chattering.

"You idiot!" Jasmine shouted. "You complete idiot!"

But Nadia shot her a look that silenced her. Jasmine felt tears prickling at her eyelids. Manu had ruined everything. She would never be allowed to keep Mistletoe now.

Chapter Eight
Harrison Meets Mistletoe

However much Jasmine protested, Mum wouldn't budge.

"It's just not safe. You can't watch him all the time, and Manu clearly doesn't understand that animals aren't toys. You have to take Mistletoe back to Honey Farm."

"But that's so unfair!"

"I'm sorry, Jasmine, but we can't trust Manu around him. And Harrison's coming this afternoon. I'm not risking him getting kicked by a donkey."

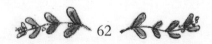

"He wouldn't! Mistletoe's the sweetest donkey ever. He just got spooked by Manu being such an idiot. And he didn't even do anything bad. He just tried to get away from Manu, which is totally understandable."

"Maybe," said Mum. "But I'm responsible for Harrison while he's here and I can't take the risk."

"So we have to take him back right now?"

"Well, not this minute. He needs to calm down first. But you or Tom must be in the orchard the entire time, OK? And, Manu, you are not allowed in there under any circumstances."

"I wouldn't anyway," Manu said. "That donkey's vicious. And it's got fleas."

"He has not," said Jasmine indignantly.

"He has, look. They've bitten me all over. It's really itchy."

Mum, Tom and Jasmine turned to Manu. Although it was November, he still insisted on dressing in shorts and a T-shirt. And his bare

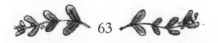

arms and legs were covered in big blotchy purple lumps.

"Oh, my goodness, Manu, you must be allergic," said Mum.

"Allergic to donkeys?"

"It looks like it. Try not to scratch. I'll give you some antihistamine to stop the itching. And you definitely mustn't touch Mistletoe again."

"I'm not going to," said Manu. "He's evil."

When Harrison arrived, he and Manu went out to the garden to make a bug habitat. Tom had to go home, but he was coming back later to walk Mistletoe to Honey Farm. Mum gave Jasmine strict instructions not to leave the orchard.

Mistletoe had calmed down now. He and Dotty were browsing in the hedge at the bottom of the orchard. His ears were facing forward and his muscles were relaxed.

Jasmine trundled her wheelbarrow around, picking up manure. In the garden, Manu was

digging a hole with a big spoon. Harrison had lost interest in digging. He stood in front of a bush some way from Manu, craning his head forward to look intently at something.

Truffle heaved herself up from where she had been lying under an apple tree. She shook her head and flapped her huge floppy ears. Mistletoe turned towards her and brayed softly. He and Truffle hadn't bonded yet, but they certainly didn't seem to mind each other.

Not that it matters any more, thought Jasmine miserably. *There's no chance of Mistletoe coming to live here now. Next week he'll be taken to the donkey sanctuary, and none of us will ever see him again.*

When Harrison heard Mistletoe bray, he looked up from the leaf he was studying. His eyes fell on the donkey. He stood completely still, watching him.

Jasmine carried on pushing the wheelbarrow. Some instinct told her not to speak to Harrison while he was watching Mistletoe.

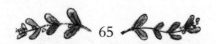

When she finished, she left the barrow by the fence. She turned round and saw to her surprise that Harrison had come into the orchard. He must have been very quiet, because she hadn't heard the gate opening or closing.

He was walking slowly down the orchard, keeping close to the hedge, watching Mistletoe, who was grazing in the far corner. When Harrison reached the bottom of the orchard, he stood still, looking intently at the donkey on the opposite side.

Mistletoe appeared to be grazing, but Jasmine could see that this was what Mr Hobson called "sham grazing". He was only pretending to eat the grass. His ears were trained on Harrison.

After a while, Mistletoe lifted his head and started to amble towards the boy.

He stopped in front of him and looked straight at him. Harrison returned his gaze.

Jasmine stayed motionless. The boy and the donkey stood completely still, looking into each other's eyes.

Then Harrison reached out and touched Mistletoe's face. Jasmine tensed, ready to intervene if necessary. She wondered if she should move closer, but she didn't want to ruin the moment.

Slowly and gently, Harrison started to stroke Mistletoe's face. As he stroked him, he began singing quietly to the donkey. Mistletoe was listening. His ears were pointed towards Harrison and his body language was relaxed.

For several minutes, Harrison stood there, singing softly and stroking the donkey's face and ears. Then Mistletoe bent and sniffed Harrison's shoes. Harrison giggled. Mistletoe's ears flattened and he took a step backwards. Harrison stood rigid, looking anxious. He waited a few seconds and then he took another step towards the donkey. Mistletoe stayed still as Harrison reached out and stroked him. Then he sniffed Harrison's face. Harrison bent forward and sniffed the donkey's face. Then he lifted his head and gazed directly into the donkey's eyes. Mistletoe looked back into Harrison's eyes, his ears fixed forwards on the boy.

A slow smile spread over Harrison's face. He leaned his forehead in to touch the donkey's

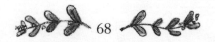

forehead. Again Jasmine tensed, watching
Mistletoe. But he looked completely relaxed,
his breathing slow and gentle. He and Harrison
stayed leaning towards each other, their foreheads
touching, for several silent seconds. Then
Mistletoe gently lifted his head and started to
amble across the orchard. Harrison fell into step
beside him, and Mistletoe kept one ear trained
on the boy as they walked side by side.

Mistletoe stopped to graze by the dividing
fence, a few metres away from Jasmine. Harrison
stood watching him. Then, his eyes still fixed on
the donkey, he asked, "What's his name?"

"Mistletoe," said Jasmine.

"Mistletoe," Harrison repeated. He stroked
the donkey's back, saying his name softly as he
stroked him.

"He likes that," said Jasmine. "You can brush
his fur if you want."

Harrison didn't say anything, but he paused for
a moment. Jasmine fetched the head collar and

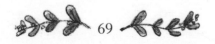

the box of brushes and combs.

"This is the dandy brush," she said, taking it from the box. "It's got stiff bristles, so we don't use it on his face or legs. There's another one with softer bristles for the parts where he's more sensitive."

Harrison didn't look at Jasmine, but he took the brush and examined it closely, stroking his fingers over the bristles.

Jasmine showed Harrison the head collar and explained what she was doing as she let Mistletoe sniff it before she put it on. Once he was wearing the collar and lead rope, she said, "There, you can brush his back now if you want to."

Harrison stroked the brush gently down Mistletoe's back.

"Good," said Jasmine. "See how he's standing quiet and relaxed, with his ears pointing forward. That means he likes you brushing him."

A car appeared on the farm track. Jasmine

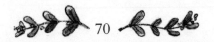

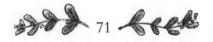

glanced round and saw it was Harrison's dad. Harrison didn't seem to have noticed. He was absorbed in brushing Mistletoe with slow, rhythmic strokes, repeating his name softly on each stroke.

He brushed Mistletoe's back thoroughly on both sides, and then, without looking at her, he handed the brush back to Jasmine.

"Do you want the soft brush now?" she asked. Harrison nodded and held out his hand.

Jasmine noticed that her mum and Harrison's dad were watching them over the garden gate. Nadia looked worried, and made a move to open the gate, but Harrison's dad said something that changed her mind.

Jasmine handed Harrison the body brush. "This is for his face, ears, tail and legs."

Harrison inspected it carefully. Then he brushed the donkey gently and rhythmically. As he bent down to groom the lower legs, Jasmine watched for any stamping or tail swishing, but Mistletoe stayed calm.

Harrison kept his eyes fixed on the donkey as he handed the brush back to Jasmine. Then he pointed to the head collar.

"We can take it off now," said Jasmine.

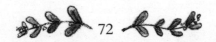

As soon as Mistletoe was free, he walked off towards Dotty. Harrison followed him, but he stumbled on a grass tussock and fell. Jasmine drew in her breath, worried he'd be upset.

To her amazement, Mistletoe stopped and turned. He lowered his head to the boy's as he lay on the ground, and sniffed Harrison's hair. Harrison laughed softly and said, "Mistletoe."

He put out his hand to stroke the donkey's face, and then he got to his feet and the two of them walked down the orchard together.

Jasmine turned and saw Harrison's dad watching, mesmerised.

He caught her eye and smiled. "Thank you so much. That was amazing to watch. I've never seen him so relaxed with an animal."

"Well, Mistletoe is very special," said Jasmine.

Chris nodded. "There's something very peaceful about him, isn't there? He's so calm that he seems to calm Harrison down, too."

"And Harrison understands Mistletoe," said

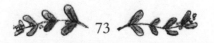

Jasmine. "He knows he likes to be approached quietly and spoken to softly. Mistletoe really liked Harrison singing to him."

When his dad told Harrison it was time to go, Harrison ignored him and carried on stroking Mistletoe.

"You can come and see him again," said Jasmine. "And groom him, if you like."

Harrison's face broke into a beaming smile.

It was only after they had left the orchard that Jasmine remembered Mistletoe wouldn't be coming back.

Chapter Nine
A Tatty
Brown Envelope

Harrison's mum phoned on the following
Saturday morning as Jasmine and her parents
were having their breakfast. Manu had already
left to spend the day with Ben.

"Sarah said Harrison was happy all day after
he'd met Mistletoe," said Nadia when she came
off the phone. "They asked him why he likes
Mistletoe so much and he said it's because he's
kind, and his fur is soft. Sarah said he had the
best night's sleep he's had in months."

"Well, it's nice that *some* people appreciate

Mistletoe," said Jasmine, squeezing syrup over her pancake, "instead of banning him from the farm and sending him to an orphanage."

"A sanctuary," said Dad. "And we're not sending him. He's not ours to send."

"Sarah asked if he could come again next weekend," said Mum. "I had to tell her that Mistletoe wouldn't be here."

"That's a shame," said Jasmine, glancing at her mum. Was it her imagination, or did Mum sound a bit regretful?

"Harrison and Mistletoe are forming a real bond," said Jasmine. "It would have been nice for Harrison to see him more. And Dotty was getting so much better, and Truffle was starting to bond with him, too. They'll be really depressed again now."

"All right, Jasmine, that's enough," said Mum.

"And poor Mr Hobson," Jasmine continued. "It will probably break his heart. If Mistletoe lived here, we could bring Mr Hobson to visit. But now they'll never see each other again, all because of you and your meanness."

"Jasmine, you've got a pig and a deer in the orchard already," said Mum. "Now you want a donkey. What next? Am I going to look out of the window one morning and see a giraffe grazing the garden?"

"That would be so cool. Where can I get a giraffe?"

Mum ignored this. "Donkeys have very long lives, you know. They can live until they're fifty."

"What are you saying? That I should only have pets with short life spans in case I get bored of them?"

"No, of course not. You're brilliant at looking after your animals. However awful the weather is, however tired you are, you never neglect them."

"So what's the problem, then? Because you can't blame Manu any more."

Mum and Dad had had a talk with Manu about Mistletoe. What with the fright he had suffered when Mistletoe had bolted, and the nastiness of his allergic reaction, he was adamant that he wanted nothing more to do with the donkey. And, for once, they all believed him.

"Well, for one thing, we don't have infinite space or money," said Dad.

"We've got plenty of space for a donkey. And Mistletoe can be my Christmas present. Which is great for you, because he's free. You'd actually be *making* money. His equipment must be worth loads. He only needs food, and we have

 78

that already."

"And a stable."

"A three-sided shelter is fine. It doesn't have to be fancy."

"It's still expensive. It needs flooring and electricity, for a start."

"And then there's the farrier's visits," said Mum. "And he'll need regular dental treatment, especially given his age."

The doorbell rang. "That'll be Tom," said Jasmine, standing up. "We're taking Dotty and Sky to see Mistletoe. We need to make the most of it, since you're sending him away on Monday."

The next day was Jasmine's final day with Mistletoe. Mum and Dad were going to help Mr Hobson clear out his farm buildings, so they gave her a lift to Honey Farm. Dotty and Sky rode in the back of the truck. Manu came along to help, though Jasmine had serious doubts about how much use he would be. Tom had had to go

and visit his cousins, so he had
said a sad goodbye to Mistletoe
yesterday.

Mr Hobson was in the donkey's
field when they arrived. Manu's eyes
lit up at the sight of the mobility
scooter.

"That is so cool," he said, as Mr
Hobson drove towards them, Mistletoe
walking beside him. "I want one."

"You can have one," said Dad. "For
your ninetieth birthday."

Mr Hobson greeted them all
warmly. "You must be so proud of
Jasmine," he said. "She's a natural
with Mistletoe. He's really enjoyed
having her and Tom around. And
he loves young Dotty, too. He's like
a foal again when he's with her."

Mistletoe bent to sniff Dotty's nose. Then Dotty set off at a run, and Mistletoe trotted after her. Sky ran along the hedgerow, sniffing for rabbits.

Jasmine headed to the barn to muck out. When she finished, she was surprised to see Mum and Dad still talking with Mr Hobson. Manu had clearly got bored, and was poking around in the hedge with a stick. Mistletoe had returned to Mr Hobson's side, and Dotty was grazing beside him.

Jasmine fetched the head collar and lead rope. "Shall I tie him to the holding ring in the barn while I groom him?" she asked.

"No, I'll hold the rope," said Mr Hobson. "I want to spend as much time as I can with him today."

He reached up to scratch Mistletoe behind the ears. The donkey leaned his head towards him. For a few moments, the old man and the donkey stayed completely still, their eyes closed and their heads touching.

Jasmine felt tears prickle behind her eyelids. She couldn't bear to think of Mistletoe being loaded up into a horsebox and driven away.

 82

She glanced at her parents. They looked sad too. *So they should*, she thought.

Eventually her dad broke the silence. "Is it just the granary that needs clearing out, Ted? Or is there anything else you want rid of?"

"Probably best if I come and show you," said Mr Hobson. "Will you be all right for a minute, Jasmine? I'll be back shortly."

"Sure," said Jasmine. "I'll do the poo-picking."

"Are you coming with us, Manu?" asked Dad.

But Manu had found a gap big enough to crawl into, and was busy exploring the hollow section in the middle of the hedge.

Mr Hobson hadn't returned when Jasmine finished, so she put on Mistletoe's head collar and tied the rope to the ring outside the barn. By the time she had groomed the donkey, Mr Hobson still hadn't returned, so she untied him and played with Sky while Mistletoe and Dotty grazed together.

It was lunchtime, and she was beginning to

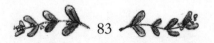

feel very hungry, when she heard Mr Hobson's scooter approaching the gate. Her parents walked beside him.

"Have you finished?" she asked as they came towards her.

"We've barely started," said Dad. "We got a bit caught up talking."

Mr Hobson smiled at Jasmine. He reached into the pocket of his tweed jacket.

"Here you are," he said, handing her a tatty brown envelope.

"What is it?"

"Open it and see," he said, his eyes sparkling.

Jasmine pulled out a small blue booklet. Stamped on the cover in silver lettering were the words:

DONKEY BREED SOCIETY

EQUINE PASSPORT

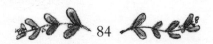

"You'll need to get it updated within thirty days," said Mr Hobson, "with the new owner's details."

Jasmine stared at him. Then she stared at her parents. They were smiling. Did this really mean what she hoped it meant?

"That means your details, Jasmine," said Mum.

"My…? You mean…?"

"Yes. I know we've been resisting, but we completely trust you to put in the work. And you clearly have a talent for working with donkeys."

Jasmine felt dazed. "I can keep Mistletoe?"

"You can keep Mistletoe," said Dad. "Mr Hobson's already phoned the sanctuary to let them know. You're his owner now."

A wave of joy surged over Jasmine. "Oh, thank you! Thank you so much."

"Thank Mr Hobson, not us. He persuaded us to let you have him, and he's insisted on paying for the shelter."

Jasmine turned to Mr Hobson. "Oh, you shouldn't do that," she began, but he held up his hand to stop her.

"I insisted. It was breaking my heart to think of being parted from Mistletoe forever. It's lovely to know he'll be staying in the village. And he couldn't be in better hands."

"He'll still be your donkey too," said Jasmine. "You can come and see him every week. He belongs to both of us now."

Chapter Ten
A Surprise

Dad built a shelter in the orchard, and when Mr Hobson moved to Holly Tree House, Mistletoe moved to Oak Tree Farm. Right from the start, Dotty slept in the new shelter with the donkey. And on the third morning after Mistletoe's arrival, Jasmine was thrilled to see Truffle there too, lying on her side in the straw, looking utterly content. That afternoon, Jasmine took away the dividing fence. There was no need for it any more; the animals were perfectly happy together.

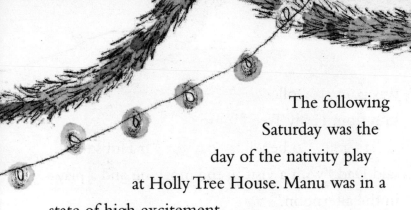

The following
Saturday was the
day of the nativity play
at Holly Tree House. Manu was in a
state of high excitement.

"Finally," he said, through a mouthful of cereal.
"Finally we get to wear the donkey costume.
We're going to be the best donkey ever. And
we're swapping so I can be the front end."

"How come?" asked Dad.

"Because I wanted to have the head on, and
Ben said he wanted to be the back legs anyway,
because donkeys kick with their back legs. I bet
they kick with their front legs too, though."

Mum and Dad shot each other alarmed looks.

"You will be sensible in the donkey costume,
won't you?" said Nadia.

"Course I will. I'm always sensible."

Jasmine was excited, too, but for a different
reason. Mr Hobson was coming to visit
Mistletoe for the first time this morning. Nadia

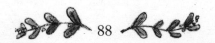

was going to collect
him from Holly Tree House.

"It's going to be a busy day for Mr Hobson,"
said Dad, "with a visit in the morning and a play
in the afternoon."

Jasmine and Tom had decorated the shelter
with tinsel and fairy lights. They groomed
Mistletoe until his coat shone.

"There," Tom said, putting down the brush. "Mr Hobson's going to be so happy to see you again."

The orchard gate creaked open and Jasmine turned to see her mum coming in.

"He's looking beautiful, Jasmine," she said.

"He is, isn't he," said Jasmine, stroking him fondly.

"I'm afraid I've come with bad news," said Nadia. "Mr Hobson's just called to say he's got a cold and he can't come out today."

"No!" cried Jasmine. "He *has* to come."

Tom looked dismayed.

"I'm sorry," said Nadia. "I know it's disappointing for you. He's upset not to be visiting, too, but he thinks it will be too much today, what with the nativity play this afternoon as well. I'll rearrange it for next Saturday. I'm sure he'll be better by then."

"He can't come next Saturday. He's going to stay at his daughter's for Christmas, remember?"

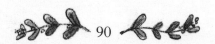

"Oh, yes, you're right. I'd forgotten. That's a shame."

"I promised they could see each other every week," said Jasmine, "and now it won't be until after Christmas."

"I'm really sorry, but there's nothing we can do about it. I'll make another arrangement for the earliest date I can."

Jasmine turned to Tom as her mother walked back to the house. "Poor Mr Hobson. He'll be so sad."

Tom looked thoughtful. "I was reading about the Donkey Sanctuary in Devon. They take their donkeys to visit old people's homes. They say the donkeys and the old people really like it."

Jasmine stared at him. "Yes! Of course! We can take Mistletoe to Holly Tree House. If Mr Hobson can't come here, we'll bring the donkey to him."

"Do you think they'd let us?"

"Well, you said the Donkey Sanctuary does."

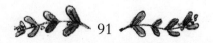

"Yes, but I don't know if all old people's homes let donkeys in."

Jasmine laid her face against the donkey's cheek. His fur was soft and warm.

"What if we didn't ask? What if we just took him? We can go this afternoon, after the nativity play."

Tom frowned. "But what if they won't let us in?"

"There'll be loads of people there. We should be able to sneak him in somehow. And if anyone from the home asks us what we're doing, we'll say he's part of the play."

"And if anyone from school asks us," said Tom, "we'll say it's been arranged as a surprise for the old people. And that's not a lie, because it has been arranged as a surprise. We don't need to say it was us who arranged it."

"Exactly," said Jasmine. "It's a foolproof plan."

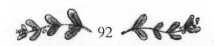

Chapter Eleven

The Pantomime Donkey

The two children and the donkey paused at the entrance to the old people's home. It was a big grand house beside the village green, set back from the road behind wooden gates.

Tom let go of the lead rein and rubbed his gloved hands together. "It's freezing. I hope Mistletoe's not cold."

Jasmine put down the bucket she was carrying, pulled off a glove and felt the donkey's back. "He feels warm. And his fur's so thick, I'm sure he's fine."

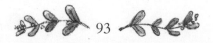

Tom looked at his watch. "We've got loads of time. They won't even have started the play yet. Let's have a look round and find the best way to take Mistletoe in."

They walked up the drive to the front entrance. It had a wide porch with stone pillars. There was a keypad and a bell next to the door, which was firmly shut.

"They'll never let us in this way," said Tom. "Let's find another door. Walk on, Mistletoe."

"It's lucky you're not a noisy donkey," Jasmine said, as they made their way along the front of the house. "We'd never be able to keep it a surprise if you started braying."

As they turned the corner, a woman in a uniform walked out of a side door, carrying a bin bag. She closed the door behind her. Jasmine waited until she was out of sight and then tried the handle, hoping it wasn't one of those doors that locked automatically when you shut it.

The door opened. She grinned triumphantly

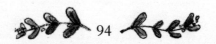

at Tom. She opened the door just wide enough to glimpse a long carpeted corridor with several doors opening off it. A buzz of excited children's voices came from one of the rooms. There was a burst of loud laughter. That was definitely Manu and Ben.

A door at the far end of the corridor opened and Ms Denby, the teaching assistant, appeared. Behind her jostled a gaggle of girls in white dresses and tinsel halos.

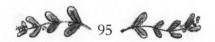

"Now remember," said Ms Denby, "we're going to walk quietly and calmly into the dining room, and we're all going to wait there until it's time to go into the residents' lounge to perform the play."

So we need to find out how to get into the residents' lounge, thought Jasmine. Mr Hobson would be there to watch the play, and they could take Mistletoe to see him afterwards.

Softly she closed the door and told Tom what she had heard.

"Let's go round to the back," said Tom. "There might be a door into the lounge from there. Walk on, Mistletoe."

Mistletoe was enjoying grazing the lawn, but he obediently raised his head and plodded alongside them.

A paved terrace ran along the back of the house, with benches placed at intervals facing out across the lawn. Two sets of glass patio doors led on to the terrace.

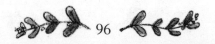 96

"I'll take Mistletoe into those bushes while you look through the doors," said Tom, pointing to a clump of tall shrubs on the lawn. "See if one of those rooms is the lounge."

Jasmine walked over to the first set of glass doors. A climbing plant ran around the door frame. By positioning herself behind it, she could look in without being seen.

It was a large dining room, decorated for Christmas with paper chains looped from the ceiling and sprigs of holly tucked behind the pictures. The round tables were draped with pretty cloths and set for tea with plates and cups and saucers. Two old ladies sat at a table in the corner playing cards. Despite the cold outside, the little window above the patio doors was partly open.

Several people wearing blue uniforms appeared from a kitchen next to the dining room. They carried trays of party food, which they set on the tables. Jasmine's mouth watered at

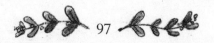

the sight of plates of sandwiches, bowls
of crisps and three-tier cake stands heaped with
scones spread with jam and cream, cupcakes,
brownies and all sorts of delicious-looking fancy
biscuits. A woman placed jugs of juice on each
table, while a man set out plastic beakers.

Jasmine remembered Manu saying the Infants
were going to have tea with the old people after
the play. Lucky them.

The catering staff finished setting up the tea
and left. The door from the corridor opened and
Ms Denby appeared with the angels. Their eyes
lit up at the sight of the food. They pointed and
grinned, and one of them started jumping up
and down with excitement. Ms Denby gave her
a stern look.

"Matilda, that is not the sort of behaviour
we want, is it? We're going to walk through the
room very carefully, and wait quietly by the door
over there. Don't knock the tables, and don't
touch *anything*."

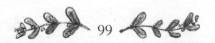 99

Matilda stopped jumping and pursed her lips tightly together in an exaggerated display of obedience.

The angels filed through the room, looking longingly at the party food as they passed the tables. The shepherds and Wise Men followed them. One Wise Man snatched a crisp when the teacher's back was turned. Ms Denby started lining up the angels by a door on the other side of the room.

That door must lead to the lounge, thought Jasmine. *That's where we need to take Mistletoe.* Hopefully the other set of patio doors opened straight into the lounge. She wondered if they opened from the outside.

She was about to go and investigate when there was a commotion in the crowd of shepherds. Something seemed to be jostling them from behind, making them screech and giggle, but the dining room was now so full of costumed children that Jasmine couldn't tell

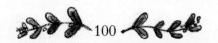 100

what was causing the disturbance.

Then she saw it, and her heart sank.

A small, misshapen pantomime donkey shoved its way through the shepherds and galloped clumsily around the room.

"Oh, no," whispered Jasmine.

"Manu! Ben! Stop!" shouted Mrs Cowan, bursting through the doors behind them. But the donkey careered around the room, kicking up its heels. Ms Denby blocked its path, but it veered to the side, knocking a table and toppling a jug. Pink juice poured on to the Angel Gabriel's white dress. She screamed and leapt backwards, sending a chair crashing into the table. A cake stand toppled over, and scones and biscuits skidded across the floor.

"Manu! Ben!" called Ms Denby. "Stop that right now! Stand still!"

She tried to catch the donkey, but it wheeled around and galloped between the tables, sending chairs crashing to the floor. Its head now hung

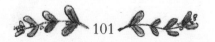

from its neck at a most unnatural angle, and it no longer seemed to have any idea where it was going.

Mrs Cowan, her mouth open in horror, wove her way between the tables towards the donkey. It turned and galloped off in the other direction. Mrs Cowan followed it, shouting, "Stop! Manu! Ben! Stop!"

The donkey turned and crashed into the
huddle of shepherds. Children dodged out of the
way as it galumphed around the room, scattering
sandwiches and sending jugs of juice pouring
on to the floor. Its head dangled from its neck as
though it might fall off at any moment.

Two of the catering staff appeared in the kitchen doorway. Their mouths opened in horror. Mrs Cowan desperately battled through the sea of children to block the donkey's way. Just as it was about to crash into her, its back legs slipped in a puddle of juice. Its front legs skidded on a soggy sandwich and the donkey toppled sideways into a table. The cake stand clattered to the floor and the donkey collapsed in a tangle of hooves, landing face down with its head in a heap of scones.

There was a terrible silence. The donkey struggled to its feet. Its face was covered in clotted cream. Chunks of squashed scone stuck to the cream like huge misshapen boils. Its juice-soaked body and legs were dotted with soggy bits of broken biscuits and squished crisps.

The donkey slowly removed its head. And there, for the whole room to see, was the tousled hair and sweaty face of Jasmine's little brother.

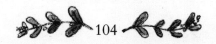

Chapter Twelve
Who's Going to be the Donkey?

Jasmine couldn't bear to watch. She walked back to the bushes and told Tom what she'd seen.

"They're going to be in so much trouble," she said. "And those poor cooks. What a waste of a lovely tea."

"Do you think they'll cancel the play?" asked Tom.

Jasmine stared at him. It hadn't occurred to her that the play would be cancelled.

"If they do," said Tom, "then we can just take Mistletoe in to see the old people now, and I bet

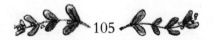

the head of the home will be really pleased we brought him."

"I'll go and see what's happening," said Jasmine.

She took up her position beside the doors again. All the children except Manu and Ben had been herded to the end of the room nearest the lounge. One of the catering staff carried the donkey costume into the kitchen. Manu and Ben stood on their own in the middle of the room, looking very subdued. The two card-playing ladies in the corner had their heads turned, apparently talking to somebody behind them. Jasmine craned her neck to see.

Harrison was crouched behind the table with his hands over his ears. The old ladies were clearly trying to comfort him, but Harrison was shaking his head from side to side and shrinking further into the corner. Ms Denby, who normally helped him, was sponging juice off the Angel Gabriel on the other side of the room.

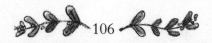

Poor Harrison, thought Jasmine. *He must have hated all that chaos.*

Then she had a thought. It might not work, but it was worth a try. She pushed down the door handle and slipped inside the room.

The teachers had their backs to Jasmine, but one of the shepherds recognised her and waved. Jasmine put her finger to her lips and crept in an exaggerated tiptoe towards Harrison. The Infants took the hint and said nothing. Some of them even put their fingers to their lips too.

Manu was pleading with Mrs Cowan. He sounded close to tears.

"*Please*," he begged. "We'll be so good, I promise. We'll do everything you tell us, won't we, Ben? *Please*, Mrs Cowan. We'll do anything."

"Absolutely not," said Mrs Cowan. "I just can't trust you. You were given very clear instructions and you did exactly what you were told not to do."

Jasmine squeezed behind the corner table and

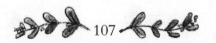

crouched beside Harrison. His eyes were screwed shut and he was rocking backwards and forwards, moaning.

"Harrison," she whispered. "It's me, Jasmine."

He carried on rocking and moaning.

"Harrison," whispered Jasmine. "Mistletoe is here."

His moaning quietened a little.

"Mistletoe is right outside," said Jasmine. "Do you want to come and see him?"

He hovered his hands slightly away from his ears and opened his eyes.

"Mistletoe," he murmured.

"Come and see him. Come and see Mistletoe."

"Mistletoe," said Harrison. He lowered his hands.

"He's in the garden, just outside that door."

She held out her hand. Without looking at her, he took it and got to his feet. The old ladies smiled at her as she led him towards the patio doors.

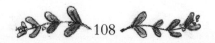 108

Mrs Cowan was giving instructions to Manu and Ben.

"You will sit on the floor at the front and watch the play. I'll be keeping an eye on you the entire time, so do not move a muscle."

"But who's going to be the donkey?" asked Ben.

"Nobody is going to be the donkey."

"But what about when everyone sings 'Little Donkey?'" said Manu. "It won't make sense if there isn't a donkey."

As Jasmine glimpsed her brother's crestfallen face, she felt a pang of sympathy. Poor Manu. He had been so looking forward to playing the donkey. She and Harrison slipped outside and Jasmine closed the door behind them, shuddering as the freezing air hit her. Harrison smiled in delight as he saw the donkey grazing the lawn.

"Mistletoe," he said. The donkey raised his head and swivelled his ears towards him.

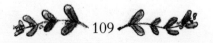

Harrison put his arms around Mistletoe's neck and leaned his head against the donkey's mane.

"What's happening in there?" Tom asked Jasmine.

"Manu and Ben aren't allowed to be the donkey any more."

"So who is?"

"No one. They're not having a donkey."

"That's a shame. It won't be so good without a donkey."

Harrison raised his head and looked at Jasmine.

"Mistletoe," he said.

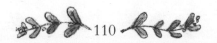

"Yes," said Jasmine absently.

"Mistletoe," repeated Harrison, and the urgency of his tone made Jasmine take notice.

"Oh!" she breathed. "Mistletoe. Of course!"

Tom stared at her, and then at Harrison.

"Do you mean Mistletoe should be the donkey in the play?"

Harrison nodded.

Jasmine and Tom looked at each other, and their faces broke into smiles.

"That's a brilliant idea," said Tom. "Of course it should be Mistletoe. Imagine how pleased Mr Hobson will be to see him in the play!"

"But how are we going to do it?" asked Jasmine. "The play's about to start."

"Harrison will need to lead him," said Tom. "Will you do that, Harrison?"

Harrison nodded.

"Right," said Jasmine. "Let's make a plan."

Chapter Thirteen
The Nativity Play

From the lounge drifted the sound of "Once in Royal David's City", played softly on a piano. Jasmine looked through the glass doors. Dozens of children were crowded at this end of the room, all facing the stage at the front. The boy and girl playing Mary and Joseph stood at the back of the crowd, just on the other side of the door from Jasmine.

She noticed with gratitude that there was a window open in this room, too, so she would be able to hear what was happening.

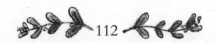

Over the heads of the costumed children, Jasmine saw the residents of Holly Tree House waiting for the play to begin. They sat in armchairs and wheelchairs, with a central aisle between the chairs for the performers to walk down. The front of the room had been left clear as a stage. A dark-blue backcloth, painted with a scene of Bethlehem by night under a starry sky, hung on the wall behind the stage.

Mr Hobson was sitting on his own at the side of the room. His face was grey and sunken, his cheeks hollow. It was sad to see him here, looking old and tired, instead of out in his field with Mistletoe. There he had been a farmer, but here he was just an old person in a home.

Jasmine walked back to the others.

"It looks like they're about to start. Let's wait on the terrace until it's time for Mary and Joseph to come on. Then we'll open the doors and Harrison and Mistletoe can walk down the aisle with them."

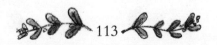

"Shouldn't we warn Mary and Joseph?" said Tom. "They might get a bit of a shock if a donkey suddenly appears beside them with no warning."

"Good point," said Jasmine. "I'll creep in and tell them."

The angels were processing up the aisle, singing "O Little Town of Bethlehem", accompanied by the piano. Jasmine inched open the door. The children at the back turned as the cold air hit them. One of the Wise Men gave a little scream, which luckily was drowned out by the piano and the appreciative murmurs of the audience as the angels approached the stage.

Mrs Cowan stood at the side of the stage, smiling encouragingly at the angels. Ms Denby was at the back of the room, facing away from Jasmine, lining up the shepherds.

Jasmine beckoned to Mary and Joseph. They looked bemused, but they knew she was Manu's big sister and they followed her

without questioning.

Outside, Jasmine shut the door behind them and pointed across the lawn, where Harrison was leading Mistletoe towards the terrace.

The children gasped. "A donkey!" said Joseph.

"He's so cute!" said Mary.

"He's going to be in the play with you," said Jasmine. "He's called Mistletoe and he's my donkey. Harrison's going to lead him up the aisle, and you can walk with him, exactly like

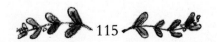

you were going to walk with the
pretend donkey. Is that OK?"

Mary and Joseph beamed.

"Can I stroke him?" asked Mary.

"Sure," said Jasmine. "Harrison will
show you where he likes being stroked."

"What if he poos?" asked Joseph.

"He probably won't, but we've got a
bucket just in case. Actually, can you carry it?
Stand it under his back end when he gets
on stage. If he moves, move the bucket
too."

"Oh!" gasped Tom. "It's snowing!"

Jasmine looked up. Fat white
snowflakes drifted like magic from the
winter sky.

"Yay!" she exclaimed. "Snow!"

Mary and Joseph laughed and clapped in
delight. "Snow!"

"Look, Mistletoe, snow!" said Harrison,
throwing back his head and opening

his mouth to catch the falling flakes,
laughing as they melted on his
tongue.

They led Mistletoe on to
the terrace, Mary and Joseph
running with their hands
held out wide to catch
snowflakes.

As they reached the doors, the angels finished singing. Four children who Jasmine guessed were narrators walked up the aisle. They wore Christmas jumpers instead of costumes, and each clutched a clipboard with a script attached to it.

The first narrator, a very confident-looking boy in a snowman jumper, yelled, "WELCOME TO OUR NATIVITY PLAY!"

The audience jumped as though they had been given electric shocks. A few people started laughing.

Jasmine turned to check on Harrison. He stood beside Mistletoe, murmuring the donkey's name over and over again. And while Mistletoe's left ear was swivelling about, listening to the noises from inside, his right ear was fixed on Harrison.

The second narrator said, "The Angel Gabriel was sent from God to a city called Nazareth, to a young woman named Mary, who was engaged to a man called Joseph."

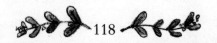

The Angel Gabriel stepped forward and said, "Do not be afraid, Mary. God is with you. You will have a baby and you will call him Jesus, and he will be the Son of God."

One of the angels was picking her nose and inspecting the results with intense interest. One had sat down with her legs crossed and appeared to be taking a nap. Another was looking around the audience anxiously. Suddenly her face broke into a beaming smile and she ran off down the aisle calling, "Nana! Nana!"

Mrs Cowan whispered to the third narrator, who lifted his clipboard and held it directly in front of his face. In one breathless outpouring, he gabbled, "In those days Caesar Augustus ordered that everyone must go to be registered in their own town. So Mary and Joseph went to Bethlehem."

The piano started to play "Little Donkey". Mary and Joseph looked at Jasmine expectantly.

Until this moment, Jasmine had been so

caught up in the excitement of their plan that she hadn't considered the possible consequences. Now her stomach twisted into knots.

Feeling queasy, she opened the double doors wide.

"Ready, Harrison?" she whispered.

"Walk on," said Harrison.

He began to lead Mistletoe up the aisle beside Mary and Joseph. Mistletoe kept his right ear trained on Harrison, and Jasmine could tell that Harrison was murmuring the donkey's name. Mrs Cowan stared, open-mouthed and speechless. Jasmine and Tom hastily ducked behind the Wise Men.

A wave of gasps and murmurs rose around the room as the little procession made its way up the aisle.

"Ahh!"

"Oh, look!"

"A real donkey!"

"Isn't he beautiful?"

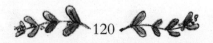

"Look at that, George, a real donkey."

"What a sweet little creature."

"Look at his dear little face."

Jasmine couldn't resist standing up to look at Mr Hobson. He was gazing at Mistletoe as though he was in a trance.

Most of the angels had stopped singing "Little Donkey" and were staring open-mouthed at Mistletoe as he walked calmly up the aisle, one ear swivelling and the other trained on Harrison. Jasmine noticed Manu and Ben, grinning in delight at Harrison and Mistletoe.

They reached the stage and turned to face the audience. The music stopped and there was a moment of expectant hush. Then, just as the fourth narrator opened his mouth to speak, a voice came from the side of the room.

"Mistletoe," said Mr Hobson hoarsely. "It's my Mistletoe."

The donkey's ears swivelled towards him. Mr Hobson tried to heave himself out of his wheelchair, but the effort was too much and he sank down again.

"Mistletoe," he said croakily.

Mistletoe lifted his head and brayed. Then he trotted off the stage and over to Mr Hobson, with Harrison beside him. He laid his head in

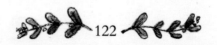

the old man's lap. Mr Hobson's face lit up in a huge smile. He rested his head against the donkey's and scratched his ears.

"Mistletoe," he murmured. "My Mistletoe."

Chapter Fourteen
The Best
Christmas Surprise

Jasmine beckoned to Tom to follow her, and they crawled on their hands and knees around the back of the audience until they were just behind Mr Hobson. He hadn't seen them yet, and they kept quiet. Jasmine didn't want to cause any more commotion. She just wanted to be close in case Harrison needed help. But Harrison was fine. He was holding Mistletoe's lead rein loosely, while Mistletoe rested his head in Mr Hobson's lap and Mr Hobson scratched him behind the ears.

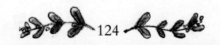

At the end of the play, as the final verse of
"Away in a Manger" finished, applause broke out
around the room. Everyone was smiling.

A woman who had been sitting at the front
stood up and walked to the stage.

"Good afternoon, everyone. For those of you
who don't know me, my name's Katy Bright,
and I'm the manager of Holly Tree House. On
behalf of all of us here, I want to say a huge
thank you to all of you, children and teachers, for
coming here and performing your play for us.
We're so grateful to you for giving us this lovely
Christmas treat. And we certainly didn't expect
to have a real donkey in our midst. Thank you so
much, Mrs Cowan, for organising that fantastic
surprise."

She smiled at Mrs Cowan, who looked rather
flustered.

"Now, even though we had a little mishap
before the show, our wonderful kitchen staff
have performed a Christmas miracle and there's a

beautiful tea ready in the dining room. Children, if you could just stay in here for a tiny bit longer, while we get all the residents seated next door, then I'll ask you to come and join us."

Mrs Cowan sat the children in rows on the stage while the staff helped the residents into the dining room. When a man came over to Mr Hobson, though, he shook his head.

"I'll stay here," he said. "With my donkey, and my helper here." He smiled at Harrison.

"You must be Harrison," he said, when the carer left. "Is that right?"

Harrison nodded.

"Jasmine told me how good you are with Mistletoe. You handled him beautifully there. With all those people around, he might have panicked, but you kept him completely calm. He really trusts you."

Harrison leaned his head against the donkey's flank.

"How did you get him here?" asked Mr

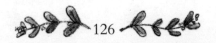 126

Hobson. "Did you bring him yourself?"

Harrison shook his head.

Jasmine jumped to her feet and came to stand in front of Mr Hobson. "We brought him," she said. "Me and Tom."

Tom stood up, grinning.

"We were sad that you couldn't come and see Mistletoe today," said Jasmine, "so we thought we'd bring him here, as a surprise for you after the play. And then Manu and Ben went crazy in the donkey costume so they weren't allowed to be in the play, and Harrison had the idea of Mistletoe being in it instead."

Mr Hobson beamed at them all. "You're a wonderful bunch of children," he said. "I couldn't believe my eyes when I saw Mistletoe walk up that aisle. I honestly thought I was seeing things for a moment. It's the best Christmas surprise I've ever had."

Jasmine fetched Mr Hobson a plate of food, but he didn't have a chance to eat anything because a steady stream of people kept coming up to pet Mistletoe and ask him about the donkey. After half an hour, he could barely speak, and a concerned-looking carer asked him if he wanted to go and rest in his room.

A Donkey Called Mistletoe

"No, no," he croaked. "I've been doing nothing but rest all week. I'm having a wonderful time."

And despite his cold and his hoarse voice, he looked years younger than he had before the play. His face was animated and he was clearly loving the attention. The two ladies who had been playing cards in the dining room made their way over. One had a little bag filled with carrot and apple pieces dangling from her walking frame.

"Lovely Maeve in the kitchen gave us these for your little donkey," said the taller of the ladies. "We thought he might be hungry."

"Is he your donkey, Ted?" asked her friend. "How come you've got a donkey, then?"

Mr Hobson told them he was a farmer, and they started asking all sorts of questions about his farm and his animals, while Mistletoe munched contentedly on his snacks.

"Uh-oh," said Tom, nudging Jasmine. "Now we're for it."

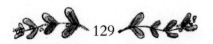

Mrs Cowan had caught Jasmine's eye a while ago, but she had been fully occupied with supervising her class. Jasmine had hoped they would be able to slip away before she managed to give them her attention. Now, though, Mrs Cowan and the manager of the care home were heading purposefully towards them.

"Hello, Jasmine," said Mrs Cowan. Her face gave nothing away. "Hello, Tom. Mrs Bright would like a word with you."

Oh, no. This was worse than she'd thought. She could cope with being told off by Mrs Cowan, but to be told off by this unknown and slightly scary person was a much more horrible prospect.

Much to her surprise, though, Mrs Bright smiled at them.

"Is this your donkey, Jasmine?" she asked.

"Yes," said Jasmine, feeling a bit queasy. "But he used to be Mr Hobson's. Well, he still is, really. He belongs to both of us. And Mr Hobson was supposed to be coming to visit him this

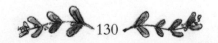

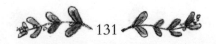

A Donkey Called Mistletoe

morning, but then he couldn't. So we brought
Mistletoe here. We'd heard about donkeys
visiting old people's homes, so we thought we'd
do it too. We didn't really have time to let you
know before we came."

"That's exactly what I wanted to talk to you about," said Mrs Bright. "I've read about donkeys visiting homes as well, and I thought what a lovely idea it was, but I didn't know of anywhere local with donkeys. But here you are, and everyone is loving Mistletoe's visit. He seems to have the ideal temperament for it."

"Oh, yes," said Jasmine. "He loves company and he's really gentle."

"We wondered if you'd like to bring him to visit on a regular basis?" asked Mrs Bright. "You'd need an adult to come with you, but if perhaps one of your parents wouldn't mind?"

Jasmine could hardly believe what she was hearing.

"That would be great," she said. "My parents are going to bring Mr Hobson to the farm anyway, so I'm sure sometimes we could bring Mistletoe here instead."

She stepped over to the donkey and scratched him behind the ears. "Would you like that,

Mistletoe?" she asked.

Mistletoe dipped his head down and raised it again. Tom laughed.

"He's nodding!" he said. "Mistletoe agrees."

When Jasmine heard familiar voices in the dining room, she grabbed Tom's arm and dragged him behind the Bethlehem backcloth.

"Hey, what are you doing?" he said.

"My parents! They've come to pick up Manu. I forgot."

"You should have dragged Mistletoe behind the curtain, not me. I think he might give the game away."

"Right, let's grab him and go. Hopefully they won't even come into – oh, no, too late."

Jasmine's parents walked into the lounge. They stopped in their tracks, looking utterly confused, as they saw Mistletoe standing with Mr Hobson and Mrs Bright.

"It's not like we've actually done anything wrong," said Tom. "We only brought Mistletoe to visit his friend."

Jasmine strained to hear what the adults were saying, but there was too much noise in the room. Then Mr Hobson spotted her and Tom

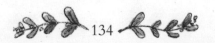

134

peeping out from behind the backcloth. He laughed and beckoned them over.

They gave each other a nervous glance and emerged from their hiding place. As they crossed the room, they were nearly knocked down by Manu, bounding towards his parents. His face was all smiles.

"Mrs Cowan says me and Ben can be the donkey when we do the play for the parents! So you and Ella will get to see us."

"Ah, yes," said Dad. "Mrs Cowan had a word with us about that. It seems it was lucky there was an alternative donkey on hand today."

Jasmine squirmed as her parents turned their eyes on her.

"These three have done so well with Mistletoe," said Mr Hobson, indicating Jasmine, Tom and Harrison. "They've given him a whole new lease of life."

"You must be very proud of your daughter," said Mrs Bright. "She has such initiative."

Nadia raised her eyebrows. "Well, that's one word for it."

Mr Hobson chuckled. "I bet you never get bored with Jasmine and Manu around. You're very lucky to have them."

Nadia smiled at Michael. "I suppose we are. All things considered, I suppose we are."

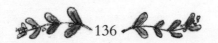

"And they're lucky to have you," said Mr Hobson

"Mostly, though," said Jasmine, "we're lucky to have Mistletoe."

Mr Hobson smiled. "I can't disagree with that," he said, scratching Mistletoe's withers. "We're all lucky to have Mistletoe."